TALKIN' GUITAR

A Story of Young ~ Doc Watson ~

ROBBIN GOURLEY

CLARION BOOKS

HOUGHTON MIFFLIN HARCOURT

BOSTON ✳ NEW YORK

Clarion Books

215 Park Avenue South • New York, New York 10003

Copyright © 2015 by Robbin Gourley • All rights reserved.

For information about permission to reproduce selections from this book,

write to Permissions, Houghton Mifflin Harcourt Publishing Company, 215 Park Avenue South,

New York, New York 10003. • Clarion Books is an imprint of Houghton Mifflin Harcourt Publishing Company.

www.hmhco.com • The text was set in McKenna Handletter. • The illustrations were executed in watercolor.

Library of Congress Cataloging-in-Publication Data • Gourley, Robbin. • Talkin' guitar : a story of young

Doc Watson / by Robbin Gourley. • pages cm • ISBN 978-0-544-12988-7 (hardcover)

1. Watson, Doc—Juvenile literature. 2. Guitarists—United States—Biography—

Juvenile literature. • 3. Folk musicians—United States—Biography—Juvenile

literature. • 4. Bluegrass musicians—United States—Biography—

Juvenile literature. I. Title.

ML3930.W28G68 2014 • 787.87092—dc23

[B]   2013034503 • Manufactured in China

SCP 10 9 8 7 6 5 4 3 2 1

4500509582

For Schellie and Patti, LaVerne, and Elouise

YONDER, where blue mountains meet the sky,
Arthel Watson was born into a world of music.

From early in the morning
till Mama sang him to sleep
at night, he listened.

He heard chickens clucking, cows mooing, the river rushing, and the high, lonesome whistle of the train. He heard tree frogs peeping, plows jangling, and voices raised in song.

Whoosh

Moo

Peep
Peep

Arthel's *favorite* music was the sound of
the wind and the rain in the trees. But he
loved the quiet between sounds, too.

Arthel had ears like a cat.

Maybe it was because he was blind.

Arthel had a heart full of melody and a head full of song. He just couldn't keep all that music inside. When he drummed on pots, Mama sent him to the porch. When he rang cowbells,

she sent him to the barn. But the music kept pouring out of him. He strung a steel wire to the sliding barn door and strummed it with his fingers.

Pappy gave Arthel a harmonica.

The first notes he played sounded like a wildcat howling.

But he kept on practicing.

Pappy made Arthel a banjo.

The first notes he played sounded like a rusty door hinge.

But he kept on practicing.

When he played a few notes on his cousin's guitar, Pappy said, "Son, if you can play a song by the time I git home from work, we'll go into town and buy you your own guitar."

That evening, with the few chords he knew
and a belly full of butterflies, Arthel played
a sweet, simple song for his family.
"I reckon we'll be buying that guitar," said Pappy.

Arthel loved his guitar, and he carried it with him wherever he went.

He listened to records on the family's wind-up Victrola till their grooves plumb wore out.

He listened to songs on the radio till Mama shooed him to bed. And he learned from everything he heard.

Pappy needed help on the farm and put Arthel to work.
Sawing logs with his brother, he memorized rhythms.

Milking the cow, he sang harmony and yodeled back
to geese calling overhead.

Before chores, between chores, and after chores,
Arthel sang and practiced his guitar.

All those chores and all that practice made him
sharp as a whittling knife and tough as a hickory.

He reckoned if he could work like everyone else,
he could play music like the folks he heard on the
records and the radio. Using all he'd learned and all
the sounds he loved, he began to make music of his own.
It felt as natural as dew on a foggy mountain morning.

Now Arthel could play what he couldn't see. He could make his guitar sound like a muskrat or a groundhog or a "wooly boogie bee." Together, they could sing songs and tell stories about shady groves, horses clomping, and catfish jumpin'.

And they could make the sound of the wind and the rain in the trees.

~ ABOUT DOC WATSON ~

Arthel Lane Watson, the sixth of nine children, was born to Annie and General Watson on March 3, 1923. Before his first birthday, an eye infection, made worse by a defect in the vessels that carry blood to the eyes, left him blind. His family lived in the Appalachian mountain hamlet of Deep Gap, North Carolina, in a two-room cabin with no indoor plumbing. His mother took care of the children and their home. His father tended their small farm and worked as a carpenter.

In Appalachia, music and song are passed down from one generation to the next. Arthel's mother sang hymns and ballads as she worked. His father played the banjo and led singing at the Baptist church. When Arthel was five or six, his father gave him a harmonica and taught him the musical scale. When he was ten or eleven, his father made him a banjo and taught him some tunes. Arthel mastered both with practice and more practice.

The music Arthel heard on the family's Victrola and radio was another formative influence. From listening to the Carter Family, Jimmie Rodgers, and other folk musicians, old-time bands, and country singers, he fell in love with the sound of the guitar. Then, when he was thirteen,

his father bought him a twelve-dollar Stella guitar of his own.

Arthel's confidence was bolstered by his father putting him to work sawing logs. "It taught me that I didn't have to sit in the corner as a handicapped person and that I could work," he later said. His earnings bought him his next guitar, a Silvertone, from Sears and Roebuck. A book that came with the instrument provided instructions on how to play with a flat pick. Arthel's brother David interpreted the songbook and pictures for him and demonstrated how to hold the pick. This determined the way Arthel played throughout his career and led to his precise, lightning-fast style of flat-picking.

Accompanied by his guitar, Arthel began playing to live audiences for radio broadcasts. At one of these shows, the announcer said that Arthel needed a short, memorable name. A lady in the audience shouted, "Call him Doc," and the new name stuck.

Doc began touring with Clarence "Tom" Ashley and his band. He also played with Gaither Carlton, a fiddler of regional hymns and ballads. Doc married Gaither's daughter Rosa Lee in 1947, and they had two children, Eddy Merle, born in 1949, and Nancy Ellen, born in 1951.

In 1960, at the Union Grove Fiddlers'

Convention in North Carolina, Doc performed traditional music with Tom Ashley. Afterward, he met with folklorist Ralph Rinzler, who arranged for the musicians to travel to New York City, to perform at the legendary concert sponsored by Friends of Old-Time Music in Greenwich Village. This led to Doc's solo career, which in turn took him to the stage of the Newport Folk Festival in 1963. There, his warm voice, virtuoso command of the guitar, and memorable storytelling were met with enthusiasm by an audience hungry for folk, bluegrass, and old-time music.

Recordings followed, nearly one album a year through the sixties, bringing Doc's unique sound to an even wider audience. He was joined by his fifteen-year-old son, Merle, a guitar virtuoso in his own right, and in 1973, they won their first of an eventual three Grammy Awards. Their popularity and success continued to grow during the twenty-one years they performed and recorded together, ending only when Merle died in an accident in 1985.

In his son's honor Doc founded MerleFest, a musical festival in Wilkesboro, North Carolina. He went on to receive another four Grammy Awards and a Lifetime Achievement Award from the National Academy of Recording Arts and Sciences. In 1997, he received the National Medal of the Arts from President Clinton, and in 2000, he was inducted into the Bluegrass Hall of Fame. He continued to perform until he died on May 29, 2012.

SOURCES

BOOKS

Gustavson, Kent. *Blind but Now I See: The Biography of Music Legend Doc Watson.* New York and Tulsa, OK: Blooming Twig Books, 2010

Metting, Fred. *The Life, Work, and Music of the American Folk Artist Doc Watson.* Lewiston, NY: Edwin Mellen Press, 2006

Watson, Doc. *The Songs of Doc Watson.* New York: Music Sales America, 1992

WEBSITES

http://bluegrassmuseum.org/hall-of-fame/2000-inductee-arthel-lane-doc-watson
Doc Watson's induction into the Bluegrass Hall of Fame

www.docsguitar.com
Biography, awards and honors, discography

www.merlefest.org
Festival established by Doc Watson in memory of his son, Merle

Special thanks to Don's Music City of Burlington, North Carolina